P9-CLR-199

Daniel Goes to School

adapted by Becky Friedman
based on the screenplay written by Angela C. Santomero
poses and layouts by Jason Fruchter

Simon Spotlight
New York   London   Toronto   Sydney   New Delhi

SIMON SPOTLIGHT

An imprint of Simon & Schuster Children's Publishing Division

1230 Avenue of the Americas, New York, New York 10020

© 2014 The Fred Rogers Company

All rights reserved, including the right of reproduction in whole or in part in any form.

SIMON SPOTLIGHT and colophon are registered trademarks of Simon & Schuster, Inc.

For information about special discounts for bulk purchases, please contact Simon & Schuster Special Sales at 1-866-506-1949 or business@simonandschuster.com.

Manufactured in the United States of America 0514 LAK

10 9 8 7 6 5 4 3 2

ISBN 978-1-4814-0318-4

ISBN 978-1-4814-0319-1 (eBook)

"Hi, neighbor! It's time for school!" said Daniel Tiger. "I've got my backpack. I've got my lunch box and . . ."

"You've got me!" said Dad, opening the front door. "Now let's get you to school."

"Please take us to school, Trolley," said Daniel as he and Dad hopped aboard.

"Ding, ding!" said Trolley.

"We're going to school today. Won't you ride along with me? Ride along!" sang Daniel.

When they arrived at school, Daniel pulled Dad into the classroom. "Come on, Dad. Let's go build with blocks!"
But Dad just stopped.

"I would love to build blocks with you," said Dad, "but I have to go to work."

"Are you sure?" Daniel asked. "Maybe work is closed today!"

Dad Tiger shook his head. "I don't think so, Daniel," he said. "It's time for me to go."

Daniel was sad. "I don't want you to go. I want you to stay and be with me."

9

"I want to stay too, Daniel," said Dad, "but all your friends are here, and Teacher Harriet will take good care of you. At the end of the day, I will come back and pick you up, because grown-ups come back."

"Grown-ups come back," repeated Daniel. He gave Dad a hug good-bye. "Ugga Mugga."

"Ugga Mugga," said Dad.

11

Teacher Harriet gently led Daniel to the art table. "Let's see what your friends are doing."

Prince Wednesday was drawing a picture of his dad, King Friday. "My dad's at work being the boss of castle stuff," he said.

"My mom is at work too. I miss her," said Miss Elaina. "But look! I have her picture in my necklace to remind me that she'll come back to get me."

Daniel picked up a crayon. "I want to have a picture of my dad too. I'm going to draw us in a rocket ship, blasting off to the moon."

Daniel imagined that he and his dad really were blasting off to the moon. *Whoosh!*

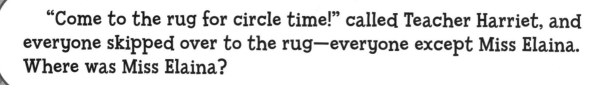

"Come to the rug for circle time!" called Teacher Harriet, and everyone skipped over to the rug—everyone except Miss Elaina. Where was Miss Elaina?

Suddenly, Daniel heard "Oh no! Oh no! Oh no!" It was Miss Elaina.

"I can't find the picture of my mommy!" Miss Elaina sniffled. "If I don't have my picture, how do I know my mommy will come back and get me?"

Daniel put his arm around Miss Elaina. "Your mommy will come back and get you," he said. "My dad always says, 'Grown-ups come back.'"

"Thanks, Daniel," said Miss Elaina. "I feel a little bit better." "We can help you find your necklace," suggested Prince Wednesday. The whole class began to look.

They looked high.
They looked low.
They even looked backward. (Well, Miss Elaina did.)
Until . . .

"I found it!" hooted O the Owl, picking the necklace up off the ground.

"Thank you, O," said Miss Elaina happily.

"Owls are excellent lookers," said O the Owl.

"Owls are excellent friends, too," added Teacher Harriet.

Teacher Harriet looked at the clock. "We spent circle time looking for Miss Elaina's necklace," she said. "It's lunchtime now. Miss Elaina, would you like to be my lunch helper today?"

"Okay!" replied Miss Elaina.

At the table, Miss Elaina passed out the lunch boxes to her friends. As everyone munched on their food, there was a knock at the door. Who could it be?

It was the grown-ups! "All the grown-ups came back!" said Miss Elaina. She was so happy.

Daniel ran over to his dad. "You came back!"
"I did," replied Dad.
"Can we go build blocks now?" asked Daniel.
"I've been waiting all day!" Dad answered, smiling.

"Thanks for coming to school with me, neighbor," said Daniel. "I liked helping Miss Elaina find her necklace. We can play a finding game too! Look through the pictures in this book, and see if you can find what I'm searching for. I'm looking for something that starts with the letter **B** on page **8**. Now find something that starts with the letter **F** on page **18**. Finally, let's find something that starts with the letter **C** on page **22**. That's great. Ugga Mugga!"